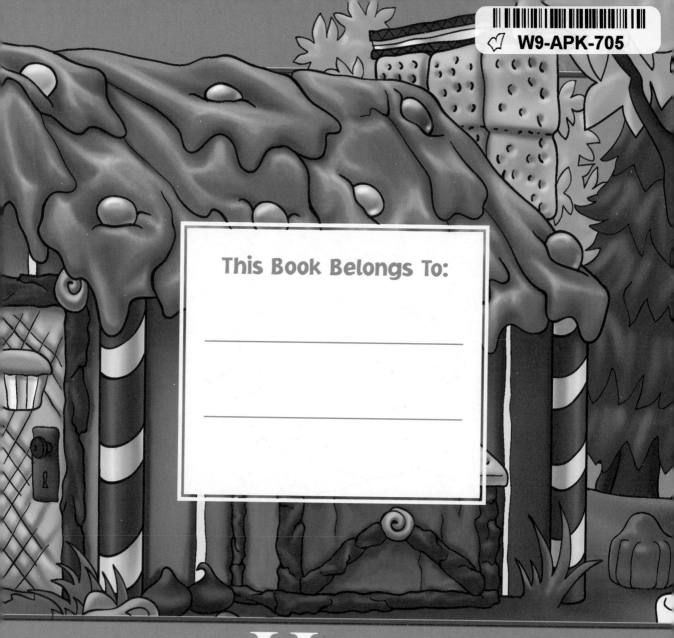

This Book Belongs To:

_____

_____

Hansel and Gretel

Once upon a time, two children named Hansel and Gretel, lived with their father and wicked stepmother. The family was so poor they didn't have enough money to buy food.

One day, the stepmother said to her husband, "We have nothing to eat but stale bread. You must take the children into the forest and leave them there, or we will ALL starve!"

That evening, the family went for a walk deep into the forest, deeper than Hansel and Gretel had ever been. Night began to fall and their stepmother told them they would have to stay in the forest.

Hansel and Gretel begged not to be left there, but the wicked stepmother dragged her husband away from his crying children. Soon, the children cried themselves to sleep.

The next morning, Hansel and Gretel awoke and decided to try to find their way home. "Which way should we go?" asked Gretel.

"I don't know, but we could try following this path," replied Hansel.

The two children walked down the trail through the trees, but nothing looked familiar. It seemed only to take them further into the forest.

Hansel and Gretel came to a clearing and in the distance saw a house that looked like it was made of candy. Suddenly, an old woman appeared on the path.

"Don't be afraid my little dear ones. I won't hurt you. Come to my house, and I will give you something warm to eat," she said.

The children were very hungry and went inside the candy house. Then, the old woman grabbed Hansel and threw him into a cage! "You, young man, will stay there, until you are fat enough for me to eat!" she told him.

Hansel and Gretel were very frightened. They could now see that the old woman was really a witch!

Gretel ran to the cage to help
Hansel, but the witch grabbed her.
"Stay away! I need you to start cooking
for your brother. We must fatten him up
so I can eat him. And once I've eaten
him, I will eat you!" she scolded.
Gretel did as the witch said.

As the days passed,
Hansel grew fatter and fatter.

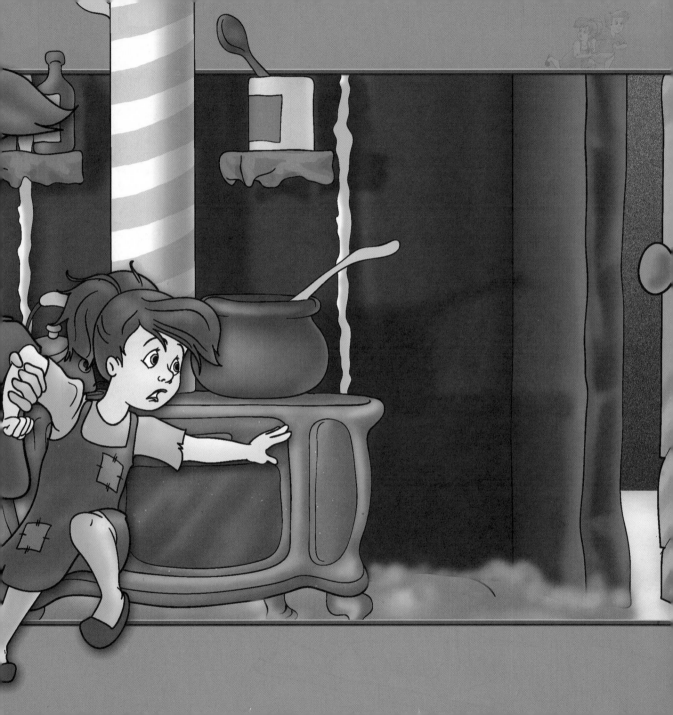

"Light the oven. Your brother is fat enough to eat!" the witch ordered Gretel.

Gretel wasn't about to cook her own brother. "I don't know how," she pretended.

"Oh, you rotten girl. I'll do it myself then!" the witch snapped.

When the witch bent over the big fire, Gretel pushed her into the oven and closed the door.

Gretel found the witch's key and unlocked Hansel's cage. "We're free!" they cried, hugging each other tight.

Just a few days before their escape, the children saw that the witch had a secret treasure. The children tossed some jewels into a bag on their way out the door. Hansel and Gretel ran away from the candy house as fast as they could. They had escaped from the witch, but they were still lost.

Fortunately, they met a kind huntsman who helped them. He knew where their father lived and showed them the way. When they arrived home, their father hugged them.

"Hansel! Gretel! I have looked all over for you. I am so glad you are finally home," he said. Then, he told them that their mean stepmother had gone away forever.